FLAMIN

FEARS &

HAPPY TEARS

AN EROTIC COMEDY

OF ERRORS

All enquiries: reallyreallynovel@gmail.com

CHAPTER ONE

Ryan – lying, cheating shit

For the past six months I had been in a proper, grown up relationship with Ryan. I was content and so happy. He was nearly everything I could have wished for, he ticked all the boxes for my Mr Romance, but after a great start the sex became unspectacular. Ryan certainly couldn't be described as Mr Uninhibited. If anything, it was all about satisfying his needs and I had to make do with digging out and dusting off my Ann Summers stash. I had tried to spice things up on numerous occasions…the man just never got the hint. I could channel my inner erotic goddess and present myself to him in all manner of positions but he'd still flip me over into the missionary position, give me a good old pounding then roll over and go to sleep. I'd managed to perfect my 'oh Ryan, you're the King' orgasm face…he may have been shit, but I didn't want to hurt his feelings. At the end of the day, the sex was regular, loving and familiar and I had begun to accept that as a lover he was never going to set the world or my fanny on fire. Despite this, things had started to get really serious. I'd met his parents and he'd given me a key to his place. We'd spend evenings snuggled up on the sofa discussing baby names…he wanted Vincent (after Vincent Van Gogh) for a boy and I had chosen Kitty for a girl. I'd put my friends on bridesmaid alert and had started looking at wedding dresses. Once we'd hit the sixth month mark, I have to admit things had felt a little different, Ryan had started to become a bit distant, cancelling dates, not turning up when he said he would. I put it down to him quitting his job and working on his art full time. He'd taken a huge step and that was bound to be stressful. I would never have imagined what was going to happen on that fateful afternoon.

I had taken the afternoon off work and decided to surprise Ryan, I thought an al fresco afternoon shag might spice things up a bit. He definitely looked like he needing cheering up and I was just the girl to do it. I let myself in and could hear Ryan grunting in the sitting room, I didn't think anything of it as he was probably painting and it wasn't unusual to hear him huffing and puffing as he immersed himself in creativity. My fanny was starting to tingle as I opened the sitting room door. Ryan was incredibly attractive with an almost perfect physique and I never gave up hope that one day he would ravish me. I imagined his face when he saw me standing there and hoped he'd be so excited he might finally let me go on top for a change! When I opened the door, the first thing I noticed was the painting hanging over the fire place, there was definitely something familiar about it but it wasn't me...unless I suddenly dyed my hair blonde, had my lips plumped up and grown a pair of absolutely fucking huge tits! I was confused and was trying to rationalise why my painting had gone when I looked over the sofa and there was Ryan...balls deep in Miss Fucking Perfection Personified!

'Ryan...what the fuck!'

The colour drained from his face as he jumped up from the sofa covering his crotch as if I was a stranger. Miss Fucking Perfection Personified looked smug and not one bit sorry for destroying my life.

‘Ann, I’m so sorry. You shouldn’t have found out like this. I was going to tell you tonight that I didn’t think things were working out.’

‘Who the fuck is this Ryan?’

‘Camilla’s Dad owns an Art Gallery and we met when I took some of my paintings in to show him, I’m so sorry Ann.’

So Miss Fucking Perfection Personified was actually a posh bitch with a rich, art gallery owing Daddy. I couldn’t compete with that could I? Why wasn’t she with Daniel, why had she impacted my life yet again…I had to ask’.

‘Camilla you absolute fucking bitch, I thought you were with Daniel?’

‘With who? Oh yes, Daniel…far too nice for me I found him terribly dull. Not at all like Ry Ry.’

Daniel…dull? Fucking Ry Ry! That was it, I couldn’t contain myself any longer. I flung myself over the sofa and grabbed her by her perfectly coifed hair. She screamed as I grabbed her and Ryan screamed as he pulled me off and realised I had a handful of her hair extensions in my hand. I may have unruly curly hair that resembles my muff more than I'd care to admit, but at least it's all my own;

'Ha! Even your fucking hair is false. What's wrong with you, can't you get a boyfriend of your own, or do you just get a kick out taking someone else's man?'

'Ann, it's not Camilla's fault. I made all the first moves…there was something about her. I just couldn't resist.'

I couldn't believe what I was hearing, he actually went out of his way to get into Camilla's knickers even though he was with me…what a twat. By this point, I'd heard enough. I pulled his house keys out of my band flung them at him;

'Here's your keys Ryan. Why don't you shove them up your arse sideways, you utter utter cunt.'

With that I spun around and headed for the door;

'…and you were shit in bed.'

I looked at him for one last time and was pleased to see his face drop when I mentioned his performance or lack of in the bedroom. As I left I heard Camilla comforting him;

'Don't worry Ry, Ry you honestly gave me the best two minutes of my life earlier.'

Fucking two minutes…he was spoiling her!

As I slammed the door on the way out it felt like I was slamming the door on my future. Everything I had planned and believed in was gone.

So here I am alone again, Ryan has messaged me a couple of times…he's sorry, he didn't mean to hurt me…what utter bullshit he knew exactly what he was doing. I deleted his messages and blocked his number, I never want to hear from the cheating twat again. It's not long until Christmas and I'm destined to spend it with my Mum and Dad yet again. There'll be no quick shag under the Christmas tree…just dry turkey ,the Queen's speech and my Dad telling endless stories of Christmas in the 1950's…oh the fucking joy! My friends have been brilliant, we've shared many a bottle of Prosecco and I think I've bored them shitless talking about the wedding I was never going to have. They have hugged me when I have cried and given me a kick up the arse when I've needed it. I need to get back on the dating horse, apparently I'm getting on a bit and time is not on my side, which is not really what I wanted to hear but I suppose they do have a point. Unfortunately I don't think I will ever trust a man again and I really should have stuck to my original plan…just a good hard fuck and maybe a cup of coffee in the morning. So no more Mr Romance for me, it's going to be Mr Uninhibited all the way! I am Ann without an 'e' a liberated, erotic goddess looking for no strings sex. If you are looking for love, don't bother to apply.

It's been a couple of weeks since I split up with Ryan and I'm starting to feel better. I'm ready to move on. I am going to be in control from now on, mistress of my own destiny. Having had plenty of time to think about where I've been going wrong, I've decided I need to be more Camilla…she's obviously doing something right, she dated and dumped the delectable Daniel and then seduced Ryan. So in my quest to become a Camillaesque erotic goddess I'm waiting to have my first ever spray tan. I feel quite excited and I got a really good deal because a trainee is doing it. The beauty therapist calls me into the tanning booth and hands me what looks like paper serviette;

'If you could take everything off and put these on I'll be back in a couple of minutes.'

It takes me a few seconds to register she's given me a pair of paper knickers…I'm horrified, my muff only does cotton! But if wrapping my fanny up like a takeaway kebab is what I need to do in my quest to become an erotic goddess then so be it. I step into the booth slightly concerned the paper knickers aren't going to be able to contain my arse when the therapist starts to spray…shit that's cold! I follow her instructions, I turn to the side, lift up my arms and open my legs. When it comes to her spraying the back of my legs, she makes sure to fill in my stretch marks which is a relief as I was slightly concerned I may end up looking like an orange zebra. Spray tan done, I get dressed and feel slightly damp and squishy. I have a quick look in the mirror and I am definitely glowing, I have to wait for a few hours before I have a bath so my tan can develop but it's looking good so far. As I'm walking home, I notice I do get a few looks…it's working already, my tanned healthy glow is turning heads…fuck you Camilla!!

When I get home I make myself a well deserved cup of coffee, I'm moving on and I'm proud of myself. I've been home about half an hour when I have a look in the mirror…fuck me! I don't look brown, glowing or healthy. I am bright neon orange! Why the hell did I agree to let a trainee do my tan? She must have used the wrong strength of tanning lotion because I make an orange look pale and I'm not exaggerating to say I look like an Oompa Loompa…I may as well give Willy Wonka a call because no other fucker is going to be interested in me looking like this. I wasn't getting looks on the way home because I look irresistible, people were looking at me because I look like the Tango man's love child. I quickly run a hot bath and I'm not getting out until I'm at least four shades lighter.

Two hours and lots of scrubbing later I am an acceptable shade of orange. This being glamorous business is hard work and I'm not sure I can be arsed! I've decided to set up my online dating profile again and I need to do some new photographs, a fresh start needs fresh pictures. I decide to go for thc doc-cycd pouty look which I had previously rejected, yes it does make me look pissed but it seems to be popular. Maybe if I tone it down a bit I'll look less inebriated. Fabulous, the more subtle pouty look actually seems to work and my photos look quite good. I upload them to my profile and I'm ready to go…again. It's not long before my phone pings with a notification…I'm fully anticipating a dick pic but I'm pleasantly surprised to see it's a message from Alex. He's the same age as me and looks very nice. I message him back straight away, I don't care if I look too keen…I'm taking control is my new mantra. After about an hour of exchanging flirty messages we agree to meet;

'I'm really looking forward to seeing you Ann and I've been thinking about what we could get up to. Are you into water sports?'

Am I into water sports? Not really, I got my 5m swimming badge at school and I don't mind a paddle in the sea but that's about it. Water sports means water skiing, surfing and water polo…doesn't it? It might be fun so I quickly hop onto my laptop and order a wet suit whilst still messaging Alex on my phone;

'I love water sports, will I need to bring my wet suit?'

'Sure, I've never tried it with a wet suit myself, but go ahead, it might add a little something'

'Add a little something?' He must be proper hard core if he does his water sports without a wet suit, I wonder if there's anywhere I can get water skiing lessons before I meet him.

'Alex, just so I know what else I need to bring with me, what kind of water sports are you into?'

'Just golden showers Ann, is there something else you're into?'

Golden showers? What the fuck is that…snorkelling in the sunlight? I suddenly get a sinking feeling in my stomach and quickly have a look at the Urban Dictionary on my laptop…Golden showers, the act of…absolutely no way, not happening! The last person that peed on me was my cousin's three month old baby…I'm sorry Alex it's just a big no from me. I don't know what to say, so I just say the first thing that comes into my head;

'Sorry Alex got to go…my cat just died and I think I'm going to be unavailable for a bit…bye.'

With that, I deleted his messages and took a deep breath…shit! What the fuck was that all about? Do you think I'll be able to get my money back on the wet suit I just bought?

Just as I'm thinking it wasn't a good idea to get back into online dating my phone pings with another message…this must be a record, no dick pics and two men interested in my profile within a couple of hours of each other. I feel like I can't be arsed after the conversation I've just had, but my curiosity gets the better of me. The message is from Leo, he's 35 and a plumber (oh the irony). He's very attractive and I might just be tempted to message him back.

CHAPTER TWO

Leo

I did it, I messaged Leo back and I'm going to give him a try. I can't wait to see him in the flesh. He's extremely fit with blonde curly hair and dark brown eyes. He looks like he could be a bit of a charmer…that's fine by me, I'm not after a life partner just a good shag and a handshake in the morning. I'm meeting him today and we're going to the beach…the beach in the middle of fucking winter, what on earth was I thinking? I would say it's quite romantic, but that romance nonsense is not for me any more. After Ryan I took all my romance novels to the charity shop, let some other poor deluded soul read them. Mr Romance is dead, long live Mr Uninhibited! I had thought about messaging Daniel, after all he had been dumped too, but I decided against it…Daniel is ancient history and there's no way I want Camilla's sloppy seconds. I imagine her talking to Ryan after I left;

'Don't worry Ry, Ry. She'll be fine, she'll just go straight back to Daniel.'

She's very much mistaken if she thinks Daniel would ever date me again… I suppose she doesn't know the history of Daniel's bellend. It left him so mentally scarred that every time he lays eyes on me he all he sees is his smouldering penis. Do I wish Ryan every happiness in his new relationship - do I fuck, I hope she tramples all over his heart like he trampled over mine! Enough of Ryan, I need to focus on my date with Leo…look forward not back. It's so cold today, I don't think I'll be unleashing my inner erotic goddess as the tide rolls in so I opt for comfort and lots of layers. My chunky cream jumper shows of my toned down tan to perfection and I've put my hair up…I can't be arsed with the windswept look today…windswept conjures up a vision of romance to me and I am not fucking going there. A quick spray of perfume and a coat of lipstick and I'm ready to go. So here I am, back on the dating horse, I just hope I get ridden like one!

I head off to meet Leo and still can't quite believe I agreed to go to the beach in sub- zero temperatures. I must be desperate, let's face it, I am a bit…desperate for a decent shag. We are meeting on the promenade next to a fresh donut stall, I'm grateful for the heat coming off the fryer and the donuts smell so absolutely divine I can't resist the temptation. I'm a bit early so a quick sugary donut before he arrives won't do me any harm. They are delicious and so moreish one donut soon turns into three. They are so tasty and remind me of my childhood, of hot summer days spent at the beach. It's quite comforting in the cold and as I'm relishing the final one when I see Leo striding purposefully towards me, he smiles and waves;

'Hey Ann.'

I can't respond my mouth is full of donut and I'm covered in sugar, he's getting closer and I'm chewing as quickly as I can, but it just won't go down. I look like a sugar covered hamster and it's not a good look. There's only one thing for it, I quickly turn around and spit it out. As soon as it hits the ground it's spotted by hungry seagulls who descend on my feet, I'm tripping over them as I try to make my way towards Leo…the evil fuckers are squawking and flapping around my legs for more. There's one (I'm guessing the alpha seagull) which is staring me down, it's tapping at my shoes for more…the cheeky fucker. I'm getting flustered as I'm trying to look sexy and seductive as I lick the sugar off my lips, battling angry seagulls is not the look I was aiming for;

'Why don't you just FUCK OFF! Sorry Leo, not you…the seagulls, the seagulls can fuck off.'

Leo throws his head back and roars with laughter as he watches me trying to fend off the angry birds. Like a true gentleman he shoos them away;

'Get away, shoo…leave her lovely feet alone.'

That sounds promising, he even thinks my feet are lovely;

'Are you ok Ann? They didn't scratch your feet did they?

He's so concerned, I might be in here!

We go for a short walk along the promenade and Leo suggests we head down to the beach. It's fairly deserted as most people are sensible enough avoid the seaside when it's wet and cold…what the hell am I doing? We walk for a bit and I must admit even though it's cold the beach does bring out the child in me. I'm happily collecting shells and hopping over rock pools when Leo suggests we take out shoes off so we can feel the sand between our toes. The adult in me thinks 'are you mad, it's fucking freezing.' My inner child however, is well up for it! I take my shoes and socks off and feel the cold sand between my toes. I notice Leo hasn't taken his own shoes off and he also hasn't taken his eyes off my feet…I think he's still a little worried that the mad seagulls took a bite out of me;

'What does the sand between your toes feel like Ann?'

What on earth does he expect me to say? It feels like sand. Has he never felt the sand between his toes before, does he have some kind of sand allergy? I don't want to offend him just in case he's had some sort of traumatic sand episode so I describe it the best I can;

'It just feels like sand really, cold, slightly damp and a bit gritty.'

He seems quite happy with my explanation and smiles contentedly as we carry on walking down the beach. We're chatting away like we've known each other for years, we have the same taste in music and films and his cheeky smile is definitely starting to make my fanny tingle. We come to some steps and decide to sit down, I stretch my legs and wiggle my bare toes;

'Just stay like that Ann, it would make a gorgeous photo.'

He wants to take a photo of me mid-stretch? Whatever turns him on! As he points his phone at me to take the picture I give him my most seductive smile. Hang on, he seems to be pointing the camera at my feet and taking multiple pictures…this is strange, why the fuck is he taking pictures of my feet? Maybe he's got a new fangled phone where you don't have to point it directly at the subject, yes that's what it will be it. I'm so behind when it comes to technology. It's getting colder so I put my shoes and socks back on…Leo looks strangely disappointed but at least my feet are warm. We get up and start walking along the beach again. Leo picks up a piece of driftwood and writes my name in the sand…hmm, we're bordering on romantic here. Not wanting to go down the romance route, I take the driftwood off him and draw the first thing that comes to mind…a huge cock. Leo looks, stops and then bursts out laughing. We also seem to share the same sense of humour…I get the feeling Leo might actually be the Mr Uninhibited I've been looking for.

We've been walking for what seems like miles when we come across some more rock pools;

'Why don't you have a paddle Ann?'

Because it's fucking freezing! What on earth is he thinking, does he want me to get frost bite? I politely decline, explaining that I don't have a towel so wouldn't be able to dry my feet. In a flash he opens up his rucksack and produces a fluffy blue towel…what the fuck? I suppose it's sensible to take a towel to the beach, but in the middle of winter, really? He clearly wants me to have the full beach experience and it's not like he's asked me to go skinny dipping so I take off my socks and shoes and start to paddle;

'Shit, Leo it's so cold!'

'You'll soon get used it, just paddle around a bit and maybe splash the water with your toes.'

This is getting stranger and stranger. As I'm paddling around I notice he has his phone out and he's pointing it at me feet again. I'm sure there's an innocent explanation, maybe he's into nature and spotted a rare starfish in the rock pool. Honestly though, it's starting to feel a bit uncomfortable so I tell Leo I've had enough;

'It's too cold, I'm coming out. I'm not sure it's healthy to paddle in the winter.'

He gets the towel ready and as I sit down, rather than hand it to me he starts to dry my feet. He rubs my feet really slowly and he seems to relishing every second of it. If I'm honest I would say he was getting turned on, when he starts to rub them more quickly I snatch the towel off him;

'It's alright Leo, I can dry them myself.'

He looks disappointed again as I finish drying my feet myself. I quickly put my shoes and socks back on and he's watching my every move. We start to head back to the promenade and Leo is chatting enthusiastically…about my feet. Apparently they are perfect, my toes are delicate and my nail to toe ratio is excellent. What do I say to that?

‘Leo I’m thrilled you are happy with the distance between my little and big toes.’

‘Now you’ve seen my feet would you like to see my tits?’

‘No you can’t suck my toes in public.’

I’m starting to come to the realisation that Leo is only interested in me below the knees. He’s less a pint of Guinness and a quick shag and more a pint of Guinness and a quick look at your feet. We get back to the donut stall where we first met and I wonder whether we will go on another date…do I want to go on another date?

‘It was so good to meet you Anne, I’ll message you and maybe we’ll meet up again…next time maybe you could wear a nice pair of strappy heels.’

With that he left. No kiss goodbye, no flirty wave, he just fucked of without so much as a second glance. It’s all become clear to me now, he has a foot fetish…he must have! All those photos he took, he’s going to be wanking over them later. Cheeky bastard, dragging me out in the freezing cold, subjecting me to a crazed seagull attack, all because he wanted to get some photographs of my feet and as for the strappy heels, he can shove those…maybe I should get a toe ring or a foot thong? Where would it end, would he want a toe up the arse? He's got no chance! I had high hopes for Leo. I was attracted to him, he made my fanny tingle but I need someone who is interested in my whole body…that's not too much to ask is it?

I call my friend Veronica when I get home. She can barely talk for laughing when I tell her about my foot date from hell;

'Fucking hell Ann, you don't have much luck do you love?'

Talk about stating the obvious! When it comes to the opposite sex I am seriously cursed. At least I'm laughing, I shed so many tears over Ryan it's nice to be able to smile again and she's organising a blind date for me. How exciting, I've never been on a blind date before and as I don't seem to be having much success (no success) with online dating I may as well give it a go. She has a work colleague who has had a series of failed relationships (sounds familiar) and he's looking to meet someone. He's called Joe and he's 31. Veronica can't speak highly enough about him. He's funny, clever and very charming apparently. She's going to message him now and try and organise something.

Waiting, waiting, waiting…it's been over an hour and Veronica hasn't called me back. Maybe he's had second thoughts or maybe she let slip that I burn bellends. Just as my thoughts turn to joining a nunnery in a remote highland village she calls back;

'Hi love, it's on!.'

How exciting, I'm going on my first ever blind date. I'm meeting Joe tomorrow, we're going for a drink at the White Hart pub. I'm to wait at the bar and wear a green scarf so he knows it's me. Shit, do I even have a green scarf? I'll need to pop into town on my lunch break tomorrow and pick one up. I haven't got a clue what Joe looks like but he's also going to be wearing a green scarf so if he's over sixty I'll be able to identify him a run. As I'm getting ready for bed my phone pings with a message from the dating site. I'm not going to bother looking at it, I'll see how things go with Joe. I may be an erotic goddess in training but two men on the go is too much for me…especially with my track record.

CHAPTER THREE

Joe

I'm nearly ready for my blind date with Joe. I follow my usual routine of a long hot bath, exfoliation and muff trim. I call it a trim, but my poor lady garden had been so neglected since I split up with Ryan that it was completely out of control. I had more bush than the Chelsea Flower Show, it was so unruly I wasn't sure whether I was going to need scissors or gardening shears. I'm wearing a short woolly dress with a polo neck and thick tights…I may be an erotic goddess but it's too fucking cold to get my tits out! I've straightened my hair and in an attempt to become more Camilla, I bought some clip-in hair extensions…I can't do the huge boobs or big pouty lips but at least I can do the long flowing locks and I still have my tan.

I'm waiting in the pub to meet Joe, I'm early as usual…I might be shit at dating but at least I'm punctual. I finally managed to get a green scarf, what a faff that was. It took me ages to find one, I'm guessing green scarves aren't the 'in' thing this winter. I decided to wear flat shoes just in case I have to make a quick getaway and I've also made sure I'm standing right in front of the fire exit. I'm watching the doors, waiting for joe…I'm excited but also a little anxious. I thought I was going to be with Ryan forever and now here I am dating again…I feel like a novice, what if I never meet anyone to spend the rest of my life with? What if I'm alone for so long my muff heals? Ok, so I know that's not going to happen but I don't want to be on my own. I quickly give myself a kick, this is not operation find a husband, it's operation get a long hard shag. The pub doors swing open and an attractive women walks in, she's wearing a green scarf (it has a couple of yellow lines running through it, but it's still green) and I wonder whether Joe has double booked…wouldn't that be typical. She's followed by a man wearing a green scarf and I wonder whether he's Joe, he looks me in the eyes and completely ignores me so I'm guessing it's not. The doors open again and a group of about eight people walk in, they are all wearing green scarves. What the fuck is going on? It doesn't take long for me to realise as on the wall behind me is a huge 'School Reunion' banner. For fucks sake, how am I going to recognise Joe? Every fucker is wearing a green scarf in here.

Just as I'm considering going home, the pub door swings open again and in walks an absolute man mountain. He's so tall and so muscular and to my absolute delight he's walking straight towards me;

'You must be Ann?'

Happy fucking days! This is Joe, Veronica described me to him so along with the green scarf (which I will now treasure forever) he knew exactly who I was. I can't take my eyes off him, he looks like a Greek God. We find a table away from the school reunion, I've already been asked if I'm Anita, Karen or Tracey and I can't be arsed explaining I'm here for a shag, not to reminisce about the time Billy Robinson called the maths teacher a slag and stormed out of the classroom. Thankfully because we have a mutual friend the conversation between me a Joe is flowing. Veronica was right, he is hilarious, I haven't laughed so much in ages. Everything about him is perfect, how the hell is he still single? I think he could be interested and he hasn't looked at my feet once. Every time he makes eye contact with me my fanny doesn't just tingle, it feels like its going to explode. The pub is starting to get quite rowdy as the school reunion is in full swing, a bloke standing next to our table burps loudly in our direction and Joe looks horrified and I'm sure he's gone a bit pale. We finish our drinks and he suggests we go and get a curry, I'm not sure if he's hungry or if he's so disgusted by the burping guy he just wants to leave. Either way I'm delighted that the evening's not ending.

As we are walking to the restaurant Joe puts one of his huge, strong arms around my shoulders and I feel strangely content. We arrive and Joe is the perfect gentleman, opening the door for me and pulling out my chair so I can sit down. I can't get carried away, he does have the making of both my Mr Romance and my Mr Uninhibited but this has to be about sex, sex and more sex. I am not going to have my heart broken again. The waiter brings our menus and Joe asks what I would like, I haven't had a curry for ages so I tell him I'll have whatever he's having;

‘Can I have two chicken vindaloo curries with pilau rice please.’

Did I hear right, did he just order me a chicken vindaloo? That’s one of the hottest curries isn’t it? I’ll just have to try and impress him with my curry eating stamina…show him there’s nothing I can’t do. The waiter brings our food and just to remind me how hot the curry is actually going to be, he also brings a jug of water to the table. What the fuck have I done…I usually go for a chicken korma and even that makes my eyes water sometimes. Joe dives in straight away and he looks amused as I cautiously prod at my curry with some naan bread…I’m going to take this slowly;

‘Do you not like the curry Ann? Go on…dig in.’

There’s nothing else for it, I take a huge mouthful and hope for the best…fuck it’s hot! I try to regain my composure as my tongue starts to burn. I smile and nod at Joe as finish my first mouthful. He knowingly pours me a glass of water and I drink it down in one;

‘Is the curry too hot? Should I order you something else.’

'No, Joe it's fine. Absolutely delicious, I'm sure I'll get used to the heat.'

Why oh why, did I not ask him to order me an omelette? I carry on eating and I think my tongue must be numb as I'm getting used to the to heat. I eat about half and accept defeat;

'That was great Joe, but I had something to eat before I came out. I wasn't that hungry.'

He touches my hand and laughs, he knows I'm a curry wimp! Joe must have an asbestos tongue as he's finished his curry without flinching once…not only does he look like a Greek God he's a curry God too. We have ice-cream for dessert which was delightful and as we are drinking our coffee I feel Joe's hand on my knee, he starts to stroke my leg and my fanny is beside itself. I feel like dragging him into the nearest alleyway and letting him fuck me against the wall. I slip off my shoe and just as I'm about to start rubbing his crotch with my foot someone on the table next to us sneezes loudly. Joe looks absolutely appalled, takes his hand off my knee and calls the waiter over for the bill. I'm starting to think that even though Joe is a man mountain of biblical proportions, he is also a tad sensitive. Sensitivity isn't a bad thing, all men could do with embracing their sensitive side and it just makes Joe even more perfect.

Joe pays the bill (I did offer to pay half but he was having none of it) and we head outside to find a taxi. As we get outside, Joe sweeps me up into his arms and kisses me passionately…I wasn't expecting that, but it was very nice. I immediately take the initiative;

'Do you want to come to mine?'

'I'd love to Ann.'

Here we go, I think it's on…I'm going to give the big man the time of his life! We jump into a taxi and my tummy starts to feel strange, it's churning and grumbling. I knew I shouldn't have had that curry. As soon as we get back to mine I show Joe into the lounge and then I go into the kitchen and have a large glass of milk to try and settle my stomach. I open a bottle of wine and take it into the lounge where Joe is nearly taking up the whole sofa. As I'm taking in the vision in front of me it suddenly hits me…if he's that big, how big is his dick going to be? I hope it's not going to be a

James mark two, I really don't think I'm up for a gargantuan cock tonight. I hand Joe a glass of wine and squeeze in next to him, he immediately puts the glass down and gently strokes my face;

'I've really enjoyed this evening Ann, you really are beautiful.'

My fanny is tingling and my stomach is grumbling…I hope he can't hear it, it really doesn't sound happy. He leans in and kisses me passionately, as he gets more excited he grabs my hair and to my absolute horror my hair extensions come off in his hand…I know I wanted to be more like Camilla, but this is not what I had in mind. He immediately stops kissing me and recoils in disgust as he looks at the hair in his hand;

'It's okay Joe, they are just hair extensions. I obviously didn't put them in right.'

He calms down as I explain, the poor man had the shock of his life. He's like a caramel toffee, hard on the inside and soft in the middle. He hands me back my hair and I chuck it over the back of the sofa…I need to work hard to get back on track now. I slide my hand up his thigh and I'm pleased to say his cock feels on the larger side but it's not so big I won't walk for a week after having sex. He starts to kiss me again, his tongue is probing my mouth purposefully and his hand has moved to between my legs…why the fuck did I put these thick tights on? He unzips my dress and I slip it over my head whilst also trying to pull my passion killing tights off. Joe gently pushes me back onto the sofa and starts kissing me working downwards from my neck. Before I know it he's unclipped my bra and he's teasing my nipple with his tongue. I guide his head downwards and he traces a line down my stomach with his tongue. As he reaches my belly button I can feel my stomach grumble, really grumble and then…..PAAAAAAARP! I don't know where it came from, but I did the loudest, longest fart I think I have ever heard. The colour drains from Joe's face and he jumps about six feet into the air as the sound of my fart reverberates around the room. Fucking hell, I don't know where to look or what to say. I scramble to put my dress back on as Joe flies towards the door;

'I'm so sorry Joe, I don't usually fart on a first date and I didn't follow through!'

‘I didn’t follow through’ what the fuck was I thinking! Joe looks even more horrified;

‘I’m going to have to go Ann, I’ll be in touch.’

With that he lets himself out and I watch out of the window as he literally sprints down the road. Another dating disaster to add to the list. I’m not entirely to blame though, Joe did order me the hottest curry on the menu and he’s so sensitive. If he doesn’t like burping, farting and sneezing it would never have worked between us. Now I know why he’s still single!

I’m just about to go to bed when I remember the message on my phone. Can I really be arsed? At this point, I feel I’ve got nothing to lose…I just farted on a first date, I don’t think it could get worse than that. I open the message and it’s from Luke, he’s a chatty 36 year old engineer. He’s written a very entertaining paragraph about himself. He likes dogs but thinks cats are twats…I agree. He’s looking for an open minded lady who’s up for a laugh…he could be talking about me and he thinks olives are the devil’s work…a man after my own heart. Luke sounds fun, I bet he wouldn’t have minded me farting at an inopportune moment! I message him back and go to bed waiting for his reply.

CHAPTER FOUR

Luke

Luke replied pretty much straight away and yesterday we met up for a quick coffee. He was the complete opposite to Joe...average height, average build and although not God like, he was pleasantly good looking with a mop of vibrant red hair. He was so funny, he made me laugh from the moment I sat down to the moment I left. He had no airs and graces and I really don't think he's offended by bodily functions. It turns out he went to school with my twat of a cousin Adrian...it's a small world! They were just in the same year, not friends which is a relief...now the handcuff joke is wearing a bit thin Adrian is looking for new dirt to dish on me. He was very sweet when we talked about what we were looking for in a relationship, he agreed with me that it should be fun all the way, but he also thought 'sharing was caring'...I'm assuming he means everything should be equal within a relationship which is fine by me. I am Ann without an 'e', erotic goddess and not beholden to anyone. We absolutely clicked and tomorrow we are going for a night away in what Luke described as an exclusive country house hotel. He's been the perfect gentleman and booked us separate rooms. If he's anything like he was on our coffee date, I don't think I'll be using my room much!

My bag is packed and I'm ready to go. We are going for a meal this evening so I've packed a pretty dark blue cocktail dress, it's about time I got my legs and cleavage out again. I wonder what the club is going to be like, it does sound posh…yet there's nothing posh or snobby about Luke at all. Whatever it's like I'm sure it's going to be fun. As I'm waiting for Luke, I can't help thinking about Joe, he hasn't been in contact since my trumping faux pas and I think it's safe to say I'm not going to be on his Christmas card list this year. I can hear a car beeping outside, it's Luke…here we go! I get into the car and Luke plants a kiss on my lips, he's obviously starting as he means to go on;

'Hey Ann, are you ready to have some fun?'

Too right I am, I shoot him a flirty look…well I think was flirty but it may well have been more squinty like I was struggling to see his face. He winks at me and puts the radio on, we end up singing along to every song together…I'm having fun already and we're only half an hour in! It's not long before we arrive, Luke pulls into the car park and it all looks lovely. The old country house is set in acres of countryside and if I wasn't anti-romance I would say it's quite romantic. Luke gets our bags out of the car and we go to check in. As we are waiting for our keys he tells me that the whole house has been given over to tonight's event…I have no idea what this event he's talking about is, but I do notice lots of boxes of tissues dotted around the place…maybe they're hosting a wankathon! Our rooms are next to each other which is quite sweet. My room is lovely, I've had the obligatory bounce on the bed and checked out the complimentary toiletries. To my surprise along with the small bottles of shampoo and shower gel there's also a packet of condoms…they clearly think of everything here. They'll definitely be getting a five star review when I get back, I'm most impressed. Luke knocks on my door and I let him in;

'What do you think of the room Ann, it's fab isn't it…you could easily fit six in here.'

He's clearly impressed that the rooms are spacious, but I think six is pushing it, there's not enough space for six beds. I don't want to dampen his enthusiasm so I agree with him;

'Oh yes, you could comfortably get six people in here.'

He looks strangely excited by this comment. He must be an interior design enthusiast…I'll ask him about that later. Luke kisses me again as he leaves my room, we're going down to dinner at 7pm so I have an hour to get ready.

I'm all ready and I have to admit I look hot…Luke is not going to be able to resist me. My dress shows off a little bit of cleavage and a lot of leg. I've put my hair (minus hair extensions, they went straight in the bin) up in an attempt to look sophisticated and I don't think I could look anymore like an erotic goddess if I tried…I'm definitely giving the perfect Camilla a run for her money in this outfit. Right on time Luke knocks on my door;

'Wow Ann, you look stunning. We're going to be in demand tonight!'

What did he mean by that, why are we going to be in demand? Does he think we look like celebrities? The dining room is packed when we get down there, it's mainly couples but there are a few single diners. The waiter shows us to our table and hands us our menus;

'What do you fancy Ann, I'm going for the curry.'

Curry? No thank you! I opt for the grilled chicken, it's unexciting but at least I know it won't upset my stomach. Luke orders us a bottle of champagne and I'm feeling contented with the occasional fanny tingle thrown in for good measure. Luke is his chatty, funny self and everyone else in the dining room seems really friendly. We are getting lots of waves and winks from the other couples and a couple of people have popped over to say hello. Luke is being so attentive, he keeps telling me how lovely I look and how proud he is to be with me. I'm convinced it won't be long before I unleash my inner erotic goddess on him. We finish eating and Luke suggests we head down to the bar. I was hoping he's want to head back to my bedroom, but I can wait. We order some drinks and Luke heads towards another couple sitting on a sofa;

‘Ann, I’d like you to meet Nigel and Gloria.’

I say hello and we shake hands, I didn’t realise Luke had friends staying here. Nigel and Gloria look to be a more mature couple. Nigel can’t take his eyes off my cleavage, it’s slightly unnerving and when he goes to the bar I mention it to Luke;

‘Nigel keeps looking at my tits the cheeky bastard.’

‘It’s because he can’t wait to get his hands on them.’

That wasn’t the answer I was expecting. Nigel was in for a long wait, it would be a cold day in hell before he was going to get his hands anywhere near my tits. I’m sure Luke was only joking and is secretly seething at his so called mate leching over me. At least Gloria seems nice, she’s chatty and I think she can tell Nigel is freaking me out as she keeps trying to put me at ease;

‘So is this your first time here Ann are you feeling a bit nervous?’

Nervous about what, coming to a hotel?

‘No. I’m fine. I’m enjoying the evening, Luke is great company.’

‘Yes, I agree Luke is fantastic.’

She winks at me and gives me a knowing look…surely she’s not one of Luke’s exes, she’s old enough to be his Mother. This evening is starting to take a strange turn. I stand up and ask Luke for a quick word;

‘Should we take the party elsewhere Luke?’

He looks absolutely fucking delighted! He tells me he has something to show me and starts to usher me towards another room. I look behind me and Nigel and Gloria are following us…fucking stalkers what’s their problem, can’t they tell we want to be alone. I ask Luke if we are going back upstairs;

‘Later Ann, I want to show you the hot tub first.’

Hot tub? I haven’t brought my swimming costume with me…shit! Luke flings open a set of double doors which leads to the hot tub room. I don’t think I will ever be able to unsee what awaited me. There were at least eight people in the hot tub, all naked and all over each other…there were legs arms and cocks everywhere. On the sofas surrounding it there were at least two sets of couples sharing the fucking love…in front, underneath, behind. I felt like I was in that film The Human Centipede as it was hard to tell where one body finished and another one started. Suddenly one of the blokes in the hot tub looks at me and gestures me to get in…fuck off! I look behind me and Luke, Nigel and Gloria are already naked. I may be a bit slow on the uptake, but it finally hits me…he's brought me to a swingers hotel! I'm so stupid, he dropped enough hints 'sharing is caring', 'we are going to be in demand' and then there were the tissues everywhere…I was right, it is a wankathon of sorts. Luke jumps into the hot tub;

'Come on in Ann, the water is lovely.'

Of course it is…the water is steaming stew of bodily secretions and you couldn't pay me enough money to get in there;

'You're alright thanks Luke, why the fuck did you not tell me you were bringing me to a swingers night…you're not friends with Andrew by any chance are you?

'I thought you'd be up for it, come on give it a try…get your swinging wings.'

‘Thanks, but no thanks. I like my men one at a time. Thanks for dinner, I’ll make my own way home.’

As I turn around to flounce out I see a flash of pink in the corner of my eye. I look back and she’s there, standing watching in the corner…the flamingo. She’s staring at me intently and even though her face is covered by the flamingo mask, there’s something familiar about her. I think she’s see the flicker of recognition in my eyes as she quickly disappears into another room. I’m half tempted to follow her but fuck knows what I might see and I’ve had more than enough for one evening. I get back to my room, pack my bag and call a taxi…what a fucking evening. I need to change my dating profile when I get back…no swingers, doggers, hot wax, feet, horse whips, handcuffs, mothers or unfaithful shits!

I’m home, well that’s another tale to tell the Grandchildren…or maybe not! I seriously am losing all faith in men, what’s wrong with them? Where the fuck did Luke get off putting me in that situation without warning me, it’s Andrew all over again…I’ve got a one man muff, how hard is that to understand? I pour myself a glass of prosecco and go outside for a cigarette, there's one thing that really is puzzling me though…who is the flamingo? There really was something about her that made me think I know her…could it be Camilla, she does seems to be following me around…if it was her does it mean she's left Ryan or was Ryan there somewhere? I'll probably never find out…the swinging flamingo is destined to be one of life's great mysteries! I check my phone as I had turned the notifications off when I was with Luke. I've got two dick pics and oh the joy, the marrow man is back, but this time he appears to have a butternut squash shoved where the sun don't shine. I delete the pictures and despair in my inability to get a good hard shag…am I destined to be a bitter old spinster who hates small children but loves small yappy dogs. I am a failed erotic goddess, how did the posh bird in 50 Shades do it?

After a restless nights sleep I wake up to two messages on my phone. One is from Leo, he's wondering when we can get together again as he can't get my beautiful feet out of his head…well he can fuck off and lust over someone else's feet…I'm a human being not an instep. The second is from someone on the dating site he's called Archie and he's really good looking and he looks very familiar. I take another look at his picture and still can't place him, I definitely know him…but who is he? Then it hits me…it's only Dr Gorgeous! I can't believe it, Dr Gorgeous is messaging me, I need to see what he has to say;

'Hi Ann, fancy seeing you here. I wondered if you'd like to meet up?'

Would I like to meet up? Hmm, let me think about that one…too fucking right I do! I don't want to look to keen so wait a whole five minutes before I message him back. I've invited him to come over to mine for a meal…shit, do I look too keen. It's not as if we haven't met and lets face it, he has already seen my fanny!

CHAPTER FIVE

Archie

I'm pleased to report Dr Gorgeous, sorry Archie is coming round tonight! I've a had a couple of days to prepare and the first thing I did was dig all my erotica novels out of the bin for a spot of revision. After the Luke incident, I threw them all away…the cheeky bastard never messaged me to apologise. Like Andrew, he probably got it on with the flamingo after I left. I really wish I knew who she was. It's been bugging me so much, there was something about her eyes and I just can't put my finger on it. I've got a bumper delivery coming this morning…a black basque and a little surprise for Archie. I've got a chicken casserole in my slow cooker (I am nothing if not organised) and I can spend the rest of the day transforming myself into a sexually liberated erotic goddess. I've got a good feeling about Archie, it feels like it was always meant to be and all the other disasters I've had were a practise run for the real thing.

I've spent the day reading and preparing for Archie. The postman came and gave me one of his cheeky knowing winks as he delivered my parcel, so I'm all set. The black basque is amazing, it perks my tits up no end and covers my arse to perfection and Archie is going to love his surprise. I'm wearing a shortish skirt and a low cut top…I've got to make the most of my enhanced cleavage after all. I've left my hair curly and my make up is natural. I'm nervous and excited at the same time and when the doorbell rings I nearly jump out of my skin. I compose myself and answer the door and there he is in all his glory…he's so handsome and with the winter sun shining behind him he looks like he's cloaked in a halo of light…he look almost biblical. He hands me a beautiful bunch of flowers and I feel myself go weak at the knees;

'Hi Ann, good to see you somewhere that's not the hospital.'

I giggle like a school girl and then blush with embarrassment as I remember he knows all my secrets! I show Archie into my lounge and grab a bottle of wine from the kitchen. I frantically search for a vase, but I don't think I've got one…I pop the flowers in a milk bottle and I'll just have to hope he doesn't notice. When I go back into the lounge Archie looks at home on my sofa and he's not so big that I have to squeeze in next to him. As we are chatting away, he suddenly mentions Sylvia;

'So how do you know Sylvia, I mentioned I was seeing you tonight and she wasn't all together complimentary.'

I explain about my date with Josh and how much she disapproved of me, he laughs out loud when I tell him how she covered up my cleavage and chased me out of the house calling me a slut.

'That sounds like Sylvia, no woman will ever be good enough for her Joshy. I'm glad she put you off, if she didn't I wouldn't be here now.'

I start giggling again, did he really just say that? The idea of no strings attached sex and a brew in the morning has gone right out of the window. I'm thinking marriage, babies and a house in the countryside with donkeys in the garden.

I'm floating on air as we eat our dinner, Archie keeps complimenting me on how good it is. I think he's being polite as I'm not renowned for my culinary expertise…I'm a shit cook! We talk about out jobs, the marketing campaign for chocolate cookies I'm working on pales into insignificance compared to him saving lives in A&E. Then I start to worry, am I clever enough for him? Am I too lightweight for an A&E doctor? Do I need to be less Camilla and more Sylvia? I quickly excuse myself and pop to the loo to check my phone. I quickly search top ten intelligent conversation starters…shit this is well out of my depth but I'll give it a try. When I return to the table Archie is happily digging in to some chocolate trifle which I'm glad to say I didn't make myself;

'So Archie, what do you think is the purpose of art in society?'

He looks at me and bursts out laughing;

'To be honest Ann, I haven't got a fucking clue.'

That makes me laugh and soon we are howling with laughter together. I get up to put the dishes in the sink and I can sense Archie behind me. I turn around, he puts his arm around my waist and pulls me into him;

'I've wanted to kiss you from the first moment I saw you.'

I quickly pinch myself to make sure this is not another one of those vivid dreams I have and it's real…so what's the catch? Has he parked a swingers caravan outside? Is he really Sylvia's love child? Is he going to spill hot wax on his own bellend? I decide not to analyse the situation too much and enjoy the moment;

'What are you waiting for?'

With that he kisses me and it's possibly the best kiss I have ever had, my whole body tingles as he kisses me like he actually really means it. We head to the bedroom shedding clothes as we go, when I'm down to my basque he gently kisses my neck and slips his hand between my legs. I gasp as he kneads my clit, he definitely has healing hands! I unzip his trousers and as his cock stands erect in front of me I remember the surprise I wanted to give him.

'Just stop a minute Archie, I have a surprise for you.'

He gives me an excited smile and throws himself down on the bed. I run to the bathroom and change into a sexy nurse outfit…he's going to love this! I straighten the little hat and pump up my tits so there's an indecent amount of cleavage popping over the top of the dress. I feel like the dog's bollocks as I head back to the bedroom, I'm going to give Archie the ride of his life. I slowly open the bedroom door…I'm milking every moment of this and Archie catches sight of me. His eyes look like they are going to pop our of his head and then…he laughs a real guttural laugh that shakes his whole body. That wasn't really the reaction I was looking for and he's not stopping;

'I'm sorry Ann, you look sexy as hell. I'm a doctor and you've dressed as a nurse, you've got to see the funny side.'

I give a polite giggle as he carries on roaring with laughter. Then as suddenly as he started, he stops and clutches his chest…what the fuckity fuck. All the colour has drained from his face and he seems to be in pain…please don't tell me he's having a heart attack, I can't be that unlucky that two dates have a heart attack on me. I feel like something out of ancient history ‘beware the Ann without an ‘e’ just one look from her and you’ll have a heart attack…I’m cursed!

‘Shit Archie, should I call an ambulance?’

‘No, no it’s fine…just a pulled muscle.’

He’s a doctor so he should know if it’s a pulled muscle, but I’m not taking any chances and call a taxi to take us to the hospital. I throw my coat on and help Archie sort his clothes out. He’s really not happy about going to the hospital but I’m not taking no for an answer.

We arrive at A&E and Archie is still clutching his chest as we head towards the reception desk. Little Miss Smug Bitch is waiting and her eyes narrow in disgust as she sees me, but light up as she clocks Archie;

‘Archie…what’s happened?’

Archie begins to explain about the pain in his chest but she can’t take her eyes off the top of my head, I’m starting to feel self- conscious;

‘You’ve got something on your head.’

I haven't got a clue what she's talking about until I touch my hair and realise I'm still wearing the little nurses hat. I quickly pull it off and shove it into my pocket…for fucks sake, how did I forget to take that off, I wondered why everyone was looking at us when we walked in. Thankfully she doesn't give her usual loud run down of why I've come to A&E…she doesn't give a shit about me, she's saving the Archie the embarrassment of his sexual shenanigans being aired in public. Thankfully we don't have to wait as Little Miss Smug Bitch works her magic and gets Archie taken straight to a cubicle.

'I'm sorry about this Ann, I've ruined what was a brilliant evening, can you ever forgive me.'

He's such a sweetheart, even though he's potentially having a heart attack, he's still thinking about me;

'Of course you haven't ruined the evening, it wouldn't be me without a trip to A&E.'

He gives me a cheeky knowing smile and squeezes my hand…it's probably inappropriate to think it given the circumstances but I wish he was squeezing my fanny!

Archie has had the undivided attention of his colleagues, he's had a number of tests done and now we are just waiting for the doctor on duty to come and let us know the results. It's not long before the curtain is pulled back in one quick swish and there standing before me is my nemesis…Sylvia. She has her head down reading Archie's notes and doesn't notice me;

'I was just on my way home Archie, but I wanted to let you know everything is fine, it looks like you pulled your pectoral muscle which as you know can be very painful…you need to be more careful, what on earth were you doing?'

At which point she notices me…she gives me her famous death stare and I swear she's trembling with anger. She throws her bag down on the bed and steps towards me;

'I should have known you'd be involved…he can't resist a pretty face. You just can't leave the good ones alone can you?'

She spits the words out with real venom, she's clearly never going to forgive me for having the audacity to date her precious Josh. Archie is clearly riled by her words;

'Sylvia, I don't know what you have against Ann, but we are in a relationship and I'd ask you to respect that.'

We're in a what now? Did he really say we are in a relationship…all that stuff I said about no strings sex and relationships being shit, forget it…me and Dr Gorgeous are a thing. I'm so excited I almost miss it when Sylvia angrily pulls her bag off the bed, it's not zipped up and something falls out and lands at my feet. I bend down to pick it up for her. It takes me a few seconds to register what I have in my hands…it's a pink flamingo mask! Fucking hell…Sylvia is the flamingo! Sylvia, paragon of virtue, judgemental bitch from hell, hater of love lumps is the flamingo! I was convinced it was Camilla, never in my wildest dreams would I have imagined Sylvia was a regular on the local dogging and swinging scene. Sylvia looks crest fallen as I hand her the mask, she knows that I know and the question is, what am I going to do about it?

‘Here you go Sylvia, what a pretty mask. I’ve heard about the lady in flamingo mask who visits the children’s ward…well done you.’

Her shoulders relax as the relief I haven’t exposed her secret flows through her. She mutters something under her breath shoves the mask back into her bag and leaves without a second glance. I know she’s been an evil witch but I could never embarrass another woman like that. What she does with her minge is absolutely nothing to do with me. Good on her I say, she’s far more sexually liberated than I could ever be…a true erotic goddess, now who would have thought that!

Archie comes back to mine and we head straight to bed…unfortunately he’s still in pain so we just snuggle;

‘Archie, did you mean it when you said we were in a relationship?’

‘Of course I did, that’s if you want to be?’

‘Hmmm, let me think about it…yes please!

Who’d have though all those months ago when Dr Gorgeous was examining my muff balls that we’d end up in a relationship…this is all playing out rather well and I start to wonder what the universe is going to throw into the mix to ruin it. I suppose I just have to enjoy every moment, maybe this time my luck really has changed. I try to sleep with my head on Archies' chest…that is the romantic thing to do after all. But his abundant chest hair is tickling my nose and getting into my mouth…fuck that, I give him a quick pat and roll over onto my own side of the bed. I drift off to sleep listening to the gentle sound of his breathing and I finally feel content.

Archie left earlier this morning, he tried not to wake me as he gently kissed me goodbye…it didn't work as soon as his lips touched mine my fanny alarm clock went off and I was wide awake. He had to rush because he needed to get home and change before he started his shift. Before he left he invited me to the hospital Christmas ball…so we really are official. It's in two days so I have a lot of planning to do. My head is full of dresses, crotchless knickers and nipple clamps when my phone rings. I assume it's Archie ringing me to tell me he's missing me already so I don't look at the number. I nearly choke on my coffee when I answer and it's Sylvia;

'Hello Ann, I feel I owe you an explanation and an apology. Can you meet me at the clock tower in the park in half an hour.'

What the fuck is going on? What could she possibly have to say to me...she can't stand me, in her eyes I'm the feckless floozy that tried to seduce her little man. I'm so curious I agree to meet her. What could she possibly have to say? I quickly have a wash, brush my teeth and throw some clothes on. This is going to be interesting and I'm not sure whether or not I should be a little bit scared, this is Sylvia after all. I've put my trainers on just in case I have to make a run for it.

CHAPTER SIX

Sylvia

I'm waiting by the clock tower for Sylvia and I have butterflies in my stomach. I can't quite believe that I am willingly waiting for the mad bitch troll from hell. She did say she wanted to apologise so I don't think she's going to out me as a scarlet woman in front of the local dog walking club or threaten me with certain death if I reveal her hidden identity. She also said she wanted to explain, but explain what exactly? The suspense is killing me but thankfully I don't have too long to wait, I can see Sylvia approaching and as gets closer she actually smiles. Her eyes look softer and she's not shooting me her usual psychotic death glare. She walks up to me arms outstretched and actually gives me a hug, I don't know how to respond so stand still with my arms firmly against my side…this is not at all awkward, not at all! Sylvia gestures to a park bench and we sit down;

‘Thanks for coming today Ann, I feel like I’ve judged you unfairly and I wanted to explain. When you found my flamingo mask you could have told everyone, you could have humiliated me and ruined my reputation but you chose not to. Even though I’ve been cruel to you, you still protected my secret and I can’t thank you enough for that. I thought you were a heartless strumpet who was going to take advantage of my son and then cast him aside when something better came along. I misjudged you.’

I’m quite taken aback by this…she is being nice, how did that happen? What happened to the old Sylvia? I’m wondering whether the real Sylvia has been abducted by aliens and replaced by a clone and strumpet, where have I heard that before?…oh yes I remember, Josh called me a fuck strumpet. I am warming to the new Sylvia but what the hell do they talk about around the dinner table;

‘I met a lovely girl last night Mum’

‘Is she a strumpet’

‘No Mum she’s really lovely.’

‘ So she’s a slut then?’

Having played out that scenario in my mind, I’m desperate to laugh out loud, but Sylvia carries on with her story and it’s important that listen to her;

‘When I was at school I wasn’t one of the pretty, popular girls. I was the clever kid, the geek, the butt of all the jokes. I didn’t have many friends and when the other girls started seeing boys, no boy would even give me a second glance, but I didn’t care because I was focused on getting to medical school. That was all the mattered. I flew through all my exams and got into one of the best medical schools in the country. I also met my husband Steven, he was very similar to me and I’d say we were kindred spirits. I was his first and he was mine, we even waited until our wedding night until we had sex for the first time. We were married not long after we finished university and within no time I had Maria and then Josh. Maybe it’s because he hadn’t lived enough or maybe because we hardly had anytime alone before we had children, Steven felt trapped. He wanted to experience all the things he’d missed out on when he was studying. He became a Dad too soon and the responsibility was too much for him. He left me for a pretty young nurse and I was devastated. She was everything I wasn't, everything I could never hope to be and it left me deeply suspicious of beautiful women. I was heartbroken, my whole world had been cruelly snatched away from me but I had to carry on. I had children to bring up and a career to carve out. The moment he left I decided I would never give my heart to another man.'

Poor Sylvia I'm starting to see why she's so bitter and twisted and I can relate to her experiences at school. How ironic that years later it was her daughter bullying me for being the geeky kid. This must be so hard for her. I don't suppose she opens up to anyone, so rather than interrupt her I just nod sympathetically;

'The years passed and although I'd only ever had sex with Steven, I felt I was missing out on something and I had never been a fan of self- satisfaction. I thought about using male escorts but the thought of paying for sex troubled me. Then one evening I overheard a colleague talking about swingers…he wasn't being too complimentary but I decided to do some research and it looked like the perfect solution. I started looking into local swingers clubs and eventually found the courage to go along. It did worry me that I might be recognised so that's where the flamingo mask comes in. I chose a flamingo because they elegant, vibrant and beautiful…so as soon as I put on the mask, that's what I became. It excited me to be completely anonymous, it meant for a couple of glorious hours I could forget who I was. The first event I went to was an education, at first I felt like a spare part standing in the corner not knowing what to do, but as soon as I was asked to join in I took to it like a duck to water. It was strange at first, I'd never seen so many cocks.'

Oh my God, Sylvia just said 'cocks'…I have to stop myself sniggering.

'I felt liberated, all those suppressed feeling and desires I'd had over the years were satisfied in one night of anonymous sex. So that's where it began and now I suppose you would say I'm a regular and I'll be totally honest with you…I do enjoy it. I enjoy the thrill of getting ready to go out and I can't get enough of the sex…it is amazing! When I feel the need, I take myself off into the countryside or book myself into an event in a hotel. I'm part of a community and we keep in touch regularly to let each other know when we'll be meeting up. I love the anonymity, I'm just known as flamingo…I suppose you could say it's my alter ego. I only have to look after me own needs. I can have sex and walk away, I don't have to give a thing emotionally and I won't be let down…apart from the odd one who can't maintain an erection, I'm always very patient with them and of course recommend they go and see their GP. I've been on the scene so long now, some men specifically search out the flamingo. I suppose that must mean I'm a good shag'.

…and now she said 'shag'. I'm really struggling not laugh.

'I'm so very sorry I was so horrible to you when you came to see Josh that evening. When my husband left, I made a vow to protect my children from heartache. Maria is fine, she's as hard as nails and she has never needed me…or liked me come to think of it. I think you knew her from school, Josh said she bullied you because of your braces. Josh however is a completely different story, he is kind and gentle. He's been my little shadow from the day he was born, we did everything together and looking back I think I sheltered him too much. He has a big heart and I didn't want to see it trampled all over, when I saw you…beautiful and confident with a magnificent cleavage I automatically assumed you would hurt him…I was wrong and I'm sorry. I can see now you would have been good for Josh, he needs a good strong woman. Don't get me wrong, his new girlfriend is perfectly lovely but she's not as feisty as you. There is something about her I can't put my finger on, she reminds me of someone but I don't know who. You see, I'm doing it again aren't I? I'm getting too involved in his life, he's happy and that's all that matters…you've made me realise that Ann.'

Sylvia is being so complimentary I'm shocked, my tits have called many things but 'magnificent', I'll take that! I'm pleased she's going to take a step back from Josh's life…the poor guy has a Mummy complex and she needs to cut the cord.

'There's no need to apologise Sylvia, you were just trying to protect your child…I understand that now. You did scare the shit out of me though! When I left your house, I half expected you to run after me with a meat cleaver in your hand.'

Sylvia laughs, her whole face softens and she looks like a different person. I've never noticed what lovely eyes she has, they are deep blue and twinkle as she laughs. I suppose that's because I've only ever seen her narrow them in disgust as she gives me one of her inimitable death stares.

'I do seem to have that effect on people, but I am actually quite nice…honestly. I just have a low tolerance for any form of silliness and I'm not particularly trusting. I've put up a brick wall over the years and you've convinced me I need to start knocking it down and start to trust again. I hope you'll be happy with Archie, you make a good couple…but don't hurt him or you'll have me to deal with. You made an impression on him from the first time he saw you…that was the time you presented with swollen labia wasn't it?'

It was all going so well until she mentioned my fanny flaps and I feel myself inwardly cringe. Oh well what's a pair of muff testicles between friends and I actually think we could be friends;

‘I’m so pleased you agreed to meet me Ann. Archie told me you’re coming to the Christmas ball, you must let me buy you a drink or two…it’s the least I can do after everything you’ve done for me. You’ve made me take a long hard look at myself and convinced me that I do have to make some changes. Anyway I must get off. I’m due at the hospital in a couple of hours and then tonight I might just be turning into my beloved flamingo…as long as it doesn’t rain, I do hate being fucked in the rain.’

Sylvia saying ‘fucked’ finished me off and I burst out laughing, thankfully she laughs too and hugs me again. This time I’m less shocked and reciprocate. Well, what a fucking revelation that was! As I’m walking home I ponder what Sylvia has said. I don’t know whether to feel sorry for her or admire her. Her husband leaving her obviously had a profound effect, but she took control of her own destiny and everything she does is on her own terms. When I first saw the flamingo mask, I thought she was an erotic goddess to be admired. But she’s totally closed the door on any relationships because she’s scared of getting hurt. Maybe there is someone out there who would make her happy…they would have to have balls of steel and an interest in al-fresco sex but there could be a Mr Romance and Mr Uninhibited waiting for someone just like her. Anyway, what do I know, she comes to life when she talks about her adventures as the flamingo. Maybe she's got the right idea…she gets shit loads of sex and never has to wash dirty socks.

Of all the strange experiences I've had over the last few months, that has to be one of the strangest. I feel uplifted as I make my way home, I came face to face with my nemesis and she was actually alright…who would have thought when I first met Sylvia that beneath that puritanical exterior was a right goer! I do hope she softens up a bit now, there is a genuinely lovely woman under that terrifying exterior and I'm sure Josh would appreciate a break from her obsessive interest in his love life. So now I can tick 'make my peace with Sylvia' off my to do list, I have to make plans for the Christmas Ball…what am I going to wear? Hair up or down? Do I need another spray tan? Am I going to get a shag?

CHAPTER SEVEN

Archie - again

Tonight's the night of the ball and I'm beyond excited. I had my hair done this morning, I've had it coloured...getting too many bastard grey hairs to just keep pulling them out and it's been straightened to within an inch of its life. I was also horrified to discover it's not just the hair on my head that's turning grey. I found a grey hair growing in my lady garden...it was too late to consider a muff dye (do they even exist?) so I had to pluck...fuck me it hurt! Thankfully my eyebrows are grey free, I had them threaded so they are beautifully arched and there's not a hint of a mono-brow. I was slightly offended when the technician asked me if she wanted to do my top lip and chin whilst she was at it...what the fuck was she trying to say? As for another spray tan, I decided against it...I want to look radiant and that doesn't mean glowing like a Belisha beacon. I'm wearing a long black dress and as Sylvia said, my cleavage looks magnificent...if Archie doesn't want to rub his face in these bad boys I may as well give up. I'm wearing heels, but not too high...I've learnt my lesson when it comes to high shoes...they just don't work for me! So that's me, ready for my big night out with Dr Gorgeous, I've just got time for a glass of Prosecco and a quick cigarette before Archie arrives...he must never know that I smoke, he's bound to disapprove.

I've just about finished my cigarette when the door bell rings...shit he's early. I down my drink and hunt for a mint, I can't go outside smelling like an ashtray. I'm flapping around like a pissed off chicken trying to get rid of the smoke. When I'm convinced it's gone I give myself a couple of squirts of perfume, thankfully find a packet of mints in the drawer and answer the door. Archie looks fanny tinglingly gorgeous...he kisses me on the lips and I push the mint I'm sucking on to the front of my mouth in the hope he tastes mint rather than tobacco;

'Hi Ann, you look absolutely stunning...can you smell smoke?'

‘Thanks Archie…no, not really. It might be coming from the guy next door…he smokes like a chimney, it’s a terrible habit.’

We get into the taxi and I feel a little bad blaming my neighbour but a girl’s got to do what a girl’s got to do and all that. I don’t want to put Archie off so early on in our relationship. He holds my hand for the entire journey and I feel so happy…tonight is going to be a good night and I get the feeling I’m going to have a very happy fanny by the end of it.

We arrive at the venue and walk in together hand in hand…we really are a proper couple and I still can’t quite believe my luck. The room is beautiful, it’s been transformed into a winter wonderland complete with fake snow, icicles and Christmas trees. It’s really romantic…yes I’m allowing a bit of romance in my life. Let’s face it, I probably was never cut out to be an erotic goddess and chatting to Sylvia has made me realise if I don’t take a chance on romance I might end up too scared of rejection to even try. Talk of the devil…Sylvia is at the bar and looks absolutely delighted to see me;

'Ann, over here…let me get you that drink.'

Sylvia hands me a glass of Prosecco and as her and Archie chat I feel a tap on my shoulder, I turn round and to my surprise it's Josh;

'Hi Ann, it's great to see you again. I just wanted to thank you, I don't know what you said to my Mum, but she's like a different woman…she's almost normal. It's good to see you happy, Archie is a great guy…he's a lucky guy.'

That was very sweet of him but before I can respond his girlfriend spots us talking and drags him off demanding to know who the fuck I was…I think the words she used were 'who the fuck is that slut?' I thought Sylvia said she wasn't feisty? Poor Josh, well at least Sylvia is leaving him alone now…but I think he may have found himself the mirror image of his Mother. Sylvia clearly hasn't seen it yet, but the person Josh's girlfriend reminds her of, is herself. I put my arm around Archie's waist and he kisses me…I feel like dragging him to the nearest toilet and fucking him, but this is his works Christmas do and I have to make a good impression on his colleagues. This evening is definitely going to be a battle of mind over fanny…mind says be sensible…fanny says come and get it! Archie is introducing me to so many of his colleagues. They are all very sweet and I've got three gasses of Prosecco lined up on the bar…they keep buying me drinks and I feel awful because I'm not sure I'm going to remember all their names;

'Ann, this is Stacey.'

I recoil in horror as I recognise her straight away…it's Little Miss Smug Bitch from reception. She looks completely different…more relaxed and much more friendly. I smile and inwardly cringe as I wait for her to say something humiliating ;

'Hi again Ann.'

Oh shit here it comes…

'It's so good to meet you properly. You've only ever seen my work persona before…I don't know what it is, but as soon as I get behind that reception desk I take on a different identity. I become somewhat dictatorial and I'm so sorry I was so loud. When you came in, I couldn't believe what I was hearing and by repeating it I knew I'd heard right. It must have been a bit embarrassing for you though, especially the hair remover cream and oh my God the love balls…I haven't laughed so much as the day you walked in chiming away like the town hall clock on New Years Eve. Every time you come in you give us a laugh, you could write a book about your adventures or should I call them mis-adventures? You must let me buy you a drink.'

Mis-adventures? No, lets just call them fuck ups and be done with it. It's good to know I've kept the A&E department laughing over the past few months…if I end up in the Daily Mail, I know who to blame. Stacey hands me a Prosecco and I more or less down it in one…I needed too as everyone in my immediate vicinity now knows about my fanny fails. My confidence restored I drag Archie onto the dance floor…he's quite a mover and we are just as we are about to start smooching to a slow number, Sylvia grabs my hand…for fuck's sake she doesn't half choose her moments;

'Ann, my special friend the flamingo wants to buy you a drink.'

I think she's pissed and I'm not far behind her. She gets me another Prosecco from the bar and then hands me a shot of Sambuca;

'Come on Ann, down it I one…down it, down it, down it!'

What the fuck is going on? Sylvia has completely let her hair down, it's like she's making up for all those lost years. She's a doctor, should she really be encouraging me to drink? Fuck it, I down the Sambuca in one and gasp as the heat hits my chest…I like the new Sylvia, I like her a lot! In the time it took me to drink the Sambuca, Sylvia has disappeared…I ask Archie where she's gone and he gestures to a crowd on the dance floor. Curious, I make my way through a sea of bodies and there in the centre of the circle is Sylvia, complete with flamingo mask performing a rather enthusiastic dance routine to I will survive by Gloria Gaynor. I watch in awe as she gyrates around the circle interacting with the bemused onlookers. She seems to be singling out one particular man in the crowd and his discomfort is palpable…does she fancy him or has he been treated to the full flamingo performance before? Has the poor man just been hit by the realisation that the best shag on the local dogging circuit is actually his boss? Before Sylvia can launch into a final chorus of the song Josh appears and tries to remove her from the circle…

'Come on Mum, I think it's time to go home.'

To Josh's horror and my absolute delight, Sylvia tells him to fuck off and carries on dancing. He looks crest fallen and his girlfriend is furious. I leave Sylvia to her audience and go to find Archie, I feel like I've hardly seen him this evening. He's chatting to a short, chubby man who has the most amazing comb over…

'Ann, I'd like you to be Robert…he's one of the hospital's biggest charitable donors.'

Robert is dripping in chunky gold jewellery and his clothes although straining to fit in certain places are clearly high end designer. I try not to stare at his hair as he shakes my hand vigorously and immediately starts to talk to me like we are old friends. I warm to him straight away, he's a jolly man with a ruddy cheeks and a booming laugh. He calls a spade a spade and he's absolutely hilarious…I wonder if I could fix him up with Sylvia? He hands me a glass of Prosecco and just as I'm about to enquire about his romantic status he starts waving at someone…

'Here's my girlfriend, she's just been to wet the lettuce.'

Oh my God, 'wet the lettuce'…Robert is a scream! I'm wondering what his girlfriend is going to be like, I hope he's just like him. Unfortunately my hope is short lived…

'Guys, this is Camilla.'

I shit you not…Camilla as in Daniel, Camilla as in Ryan. She may not have been the flamingo, but she's clearly fucking stalking me. I see a flicker of recognition in her eyes as she strokes her hair protectively…she knows exactly who I am. As Robert chats to Archie, I manage to take her to one side;

'So what the fuck happened to Ryan?'

'Who? Oh yes, him. Well his silly little paintings were doing very well in the gallery and he became Daddy's new pet. All he ever talked about was paint and chalk. Quite frankly I found it boring. He wasn't paying me any attention so I finished with him. Then I met Bobby. Bobby treats me like a princess, he'll do anything for me. He's taking me to St Lucia for Christmas and buying me a whole new wardrobe for the trip.'

So basically she's going to bleed Robert dry and then move on to the next poor bastard…why did I ever think being like her was a good idea. She cares about no one except herself. I don't think she ever wanted Ryan. She liked him, found out he was with someone and then made it her mission to take him for herself…what a fucking bitch! I feel like telling Robert exactly what she's like, but he seems happy. She's putting a spring in his step, making him feel young. I take satisfaction from the look of disgust on Camilla's face as Robert squeezes her arse and tells her he can't wait to get her home. The party is starting to wind up as we chat to Robert and I'm feeling pretty shit faced…how much prosecco have I had? I'm pleased we are leaving, Camilla was starting to give Archie the eye and I'm not losing this one to Miss Fucking Perfection Personified. We head outside to get a taxi and as soon as the fresh air hits me I forget how to use my legs and I start to stumble incoherently…I need to sober up, I've got unfinished business with Archie's cock.

We get back to Archie's and I make myself at home in the living room whilst Archie makes me a cup of coffee…he seems a bit worried, maybe it was because I fell over when we got out of the taxi. I blame my shoes…you know what I'm like with shoes. Or was it because I kept telling him how much I liked him…maybe I shouldn't have told the taxi driver my fanny was tingling. His sitting room is homely and comfortable, so comfortable I could quite easily fall asleep I decide I need to keep myself awake and give Archie a surprise when he gets back from the kitchen. I take off me dress and adopt my best 'come and get me big boy' pose on the sofa. Archie walks back in and nearly drops my coffee;

'Ann! Are you ok, did you fall over again?'

No Archie, I didn't fall over I'm trying to look sexy. I think the fact I'm dribbling a bit might have taken away from the moment. I must admit, I don't feel altogether well and before I can say 'Where's the bathroom I'm going to be sick', I vomit all over

Archie's shoes. Archie manages to get me to the bathroom and holds my hair whilst I'm sick again and again. He rubs my back and talks to me gently…I feel like a complete twat and start ugly drunk crying. I'm convinced I've blown it, how could he possibly like me when I've just vomited on his shoes. I've probably ruined them and I don't think the rug in his sitting room will ever be the same again. In between heaves, I promise to pay for any dry cleaning. He's so lovely and tells me I don't need to think about paying for anything. When he's convinced I'm finished he helps me wash and takes me to the bedroom. He gives me one of his shirts and I start to cry again;

'I'm so sorry Archie…I wanted tonight to be special.'

'It has been special Ann and we've got plenty more nights to come.'

Archie leaves me to go and clean the sitting room…he's perfect isn't he? I fall asleep pissed but happy, I haven't fucked it up and Archie wants to spend more time with me…I think this time I might have actually done it. I've definitely found my Mr Romance and I have no doubt he's going to be my Mr Uninhibited.

CHAPTER EIGHT

Lessons Learnt

It's Christmas day and I'm spending it with…Archie!!! My Mum was pissed off at first, but as soon as I told her Archie was a doctor she suddenly changed her tune;

'Of course you must spend the day with Archie…ohhh we've never had a doctor in the family. I must phone your Aunty Jean and tell her…she'll be so jealous. So I'll be meeting him on Boxing Day will I? I'll tell your Dad to get a bottle of that nice whiskey in.'

My Mum comes from that generation where doctors are thought of as super human…I've earnt a shit load of daughter brownie points and she's going to roll out the red carpet for him when she gets to meet him on Boxing Day. I wouldn't be surprised if she does a curtsey on the door step when she sees him. I just hope and pray, she doesn't invite the entire family round to meet him, it's the sort of thing she would do to claim bragging rights. Anyway enough of my Mother and back to Archie. I had a hangover for two days after the Christmas do. Archie was really sweet and kept popping to mine to check on me. On the second day when I was feeling better he came over in the evening and I'm pleased to report I fucked him…I fucked him in the kitchen, in the bedroom, in the shower and in the garden shed (he caught me having a crafty cigarette and well, one thing led to another). I think we tried every position known to man and God could he keep going…Archie is definitely not a two minute wonder. When it was time for him to leave, I waved him goodbye from my bed…not because I was tired, but because I couldn't fucking walk! It was everything I imagined sex should be and he absolutely made sure all my needs were met. So here we are together at Christmas, he's in the kitchen basting the turkey…he'll be basting me later, but I want to open my presents first. I've finally found my Mr Romance and my Mr Uninhibited…I can't even begin to tell you what he got up to with my Ann Summers stash! It's taken me quite some time and I've learnt even more over the last few months.

The first lesson I learnt was never trust an artist (that may be a generalisation but I'm allowed to be bitter and twisted). Ryan built up my trust and destroyed it in an instant. He was all ethereal and arty…you can trust me because I have a soul. Utter bollocks he was driven by his cock like every other man (obviously not including Archie). He was selfish in the bedroom, driven by his own needs…that should have been a clue that the most important person in Ryan's life was Ryan. For all his talk of love and a future he soon dropped me when he met Camilla. Now that was double whammy not only was she Miss Fucking Perfection Personified but her Dad held the key to Ryan's art career…I was never going to win that battle. Losing Ryan made me feel like I should be more like Camilla, but that was wrong. Why would I want to be like a woman who deliberately uses her feminine wiles to hurt other women. Why should I change my appearance just to attract men…no I am what I am and you can like it or fuck off. I can't even get a spray tan without it going wrong, so any form of plastic surgery is completely off the table. I was never going to be an erotic goddess, but that doesn't mean I can't be a great shag.

When online dating, make sure your know your terminology. I am of course referring to water sports…how was I supposed to know he was referring to the art of peeing on each other. I really should have checked on line before I agreed to it. I didn't even know that was a thing and now I have a wet suit hanging in my wardrobe that I'm never going to use, can you seriously imagine me water skiing or surfing…no, neither can I. Which brings me on to Leo. What can say? Firstly seagulls are cunts and will stop at nothing to get their greedy beaks on your delicious sugary donuts…they really have no fear and let nothing stand between them and food… a bit like Camilla and men. Secondly, if your date asks you to go to the beach in the middle of winter be suspicious if they ask you to take your shoes off. What was I thinking exposing my toes to the elements? Why did I not cotton on when he asked me to describe what the sand felt like between my toes or when he started to take photographs of my feet? You need a man to be interested in you, the whole package…it doesn't matter if you have lovely feet. It's you as a person that matters. He was such a good looking guy with a lovely personality…if he could just extend his desire for women beyond the ankle he would be fighting them off. Leo still messages me every so often to ask if I'll send him pictures of my feet in various poses…maybe I'll send him a picture of Archies feet and see what he thinks of them!

Never ever agree to wear a green scarf on a blind date…they are fucking hard to get hold of and look far too much like old school scarves for my liking. Which brings me onto Joe, he was an actual man mountain of Adonis like proportions…he was absolutely gorgeous, witty, intelligent but far too sensitive. In Joe's world, sneezing, burping and farting just did not exist…but sneezing, burping and farting are all part of life's rich tapestry, they come with the territory. Ok, I did actually fart just as he as about to go down on me. But looking back on it, it was actually quite funny and something we could have told the Grandchildren about. It could have been worse, it could have been a flap slapper…how would he have coped with that? You have to be prepared to accept your partner farts and all…if he doesn't make some changes quickly Joe is going to have to go and live on a desert island. I still can't get my head around it, how does he cope with his own bodily functions? Does he give himself a bollocking and run out of the room every time he farts or is it just other peoples farts he doesn't like? My friend Veronica found it hilarious when I told her. She bought a fart machine which she hid in her desk drawer and set off every time Joe walked passed. It's wicked but maybe it will be a form of therapy for him!

Don't be charmed by a cheeky chappie. Luke was hilarious with a cheeky glint in his eye. He charmed me over coffee with a view to sharing me with his swinging mates. Or it could just have been I was giving out swinging vibes…I was quite flirtatious and looking back might have intimated I was up for anything…but come on, he shouldn't have made the assumption. Don't be oblivious to the clues staring you in the face…hotel in the middle of nowhere, boxes of tissues everywhere, condoms in the bedroom, random couples trying to make conversation, couples mixing and matching in the hot tub. No wonder he was so excited when I agreed you could fit six people in the bedroom, he was gearing up for us having a full on orgy. Why did it take me until I saw the human centipede in the hot tub to realise what the fuck was going on? Luke had no right putting me in that situation without warning me…never do anything you don't want to, if it makes you uncomfortable then don't do it. I may have wanted to be a sexually liberated erotic goddess but that doesn't include sharing my fanny to all and sundry. I know it's quite popular and each to their own but I'm not out to emulate Sylvia just yet!

Which brings me to Sylvia…what the fuck! I was seriously convinced that the flamingo was Camilla…after all she did seem to be following me around. Never in a million years would I ever have thought it was Sylvia. I have to admit when I first saw the flamingo mask fall out of her bag, I did for a split second feel like telling the world, but I saw something in her eyes that made me stop. I'm so pleased I didn't betray her secret. She holds so much sorrow, imagine being let down so badly by the love of your life that you vow never to have a relationship again. Sylvia devoted her life to her children and her career. The flamingo provided her with a release and allowed her to fulfil her sexual desires, she lives the life she didn't have through that mask and no one can judge her for it. I just hope that she really does start to lighten up now…I bet she had a really bad hangover after the Christmas party. She really was the life and soul of the party and I'm sure it was a revelation to her colleagues… she's got years of partying to catch up on and she made a great start. I wonder what she was like on her first morning back at work, did she walk into the A&E department high fiving everyone on the way in or did she shoot them her death stare defying anyone to mention the events of the night before. There will be someone out there for Sylvia and now I'm going to be seeing a lot more of her, I'm going to make it my mission to find him. It's strange how things turn out, I hated Sylvia with a passion…she had treated me with such contempt and I saw bits of her in every horror film I had ever watched and now…she's my bestie!

Finally, never give up hope. After all my relationship and dating disasters I was toying with the idea of doing a Sylvia. I thought it would easier to detach myself and just use men for sex…I didn't get very far with that did I? Just as I was about to give up along came Archie, my very own Dr Gorgeous. From that first time he looked at my muff testicles, I knew there was something special about him…it's like it was written in the stars and we were destined to be together. I should never have held Camilla up as some sort of role model. Miss

Fucking Perfection Personified...but was she? She judges men on what they can do for her and changes them as often as she changes her knickers...I hope she'll be happy with Robert but I'm sure she'll dump him when she's had her holiday and new wardrobe to go with it. The look on her face when he was slobbering all over her was priceless...serves her fucking right! It's not been long, but I think I can safely say Archie is 'the one'. He's the Mr Romance and Mr Uninhibited I've been searching for...I know now it was never meant to be Daniel or Tom or Ryan. It was always going to be Archie and I'm so happy I'm crying happy tears.

Hold on my phone has just pinged with a message... it's a festive dick pic and either he's really into Christmas or he's had too much of the Christmas spirit as he's put a little Santa hat on the end of it. I wish the mystery schlong a happy Christmas and delete the dating app from my phone. I'm never going to need it again and I swear, if it doesn't work out with Archie I am definitely joining a nunnery. At least now I can look back at the burnt bellend, BDSM disaster, mad Mother, defective handcuffs, anaconda dick, dogging, the Hershey Highway, O.A. Pervert, stupidly high shoes, swinging, over sensitivity and farting at an inopportune moment and laugh! I may have been shit at dating but I got what I wanted in the end. I'm having the best Christmas I could possibly have wished for and as soon as I've unwrapped the presents in my stocking I'm going to unwrap the best present of all…Dr Gorgeous.

There are three books in the 'Wax and Whips' series – this one, 'Wax Whips and my Hairy Bits' (the first in the trilogy) and 'Shoes, Blues and Erotic To-Do's' . Here's the first few pages from 'Wax, Whips and My Hairy Bits'...

Wax Whips and My Hairy Bits...

CHAPTER ONE

Me

I used to love reading romance novels, nothing modern, just good old fashioned Victorian romantic literature. It was a time of innocence, the pace of life was slower, the men more charming. A time where you didn't have to conform to female stereotypes online, where you never needed to ask 'does my arse look big in this' because everyone looked big in a bustle and no fucker was going to get a look at your arse until you had a ring on your finger. It gave me hope that there was a Mr Romance out there for us all and then suddenly it dawned on me that actually it was all a little bit dull. It took me a bit of time to realise where it was all going wrong, but then it became clear. These novels, lovely as they were, were missing one vital component...they didn't do cock.

My name is Ann, not regal Anne, just plain, boring, unexciting Ann. I often wonder how my life would have turned out if my parents had just given me that extra 'e'. I am thirty-two years old, no spring chicken and no stranger to the dating scene. I work in marketing which isn't as glamorous as it sounds and if I'm honest it bores the shit out of me. The search for my Mr Romance had led me to a succession of short, infuriating relationships where the sex had been no more exciting than a blow job and a quick shag (missionary position). I needed less Mr Romance and more Mr Uninhibited. I needed excitement, hot wax and a fucking good seeing to. I was single, more than ready to mingle and had read a shit load of Erotica so I knew exactly what I had to do in order to embark on a new sexual adventure. I wanted no strings sex, none of that emotional bollocks, just a good hard fuck and maybe a cup of coffee in the morning. I'm bored of feeling boring. I don't want to be Ann who's a good laugh, I want to be Ann who's amazing in bed, I want to be the shag that stays with you a lifetime, never bettered or forgotten.

My longest relationship had lasted nearly two years, Hayden. We met when we were both at university. I was so young and inexperienced I didn't really know what a good shag was. I lost my virginity to him after four bottles of Diamond White and maybe it was because I was pissed, or maybe because he was shit at shagging, but it was a completely underwhelming experience. There was no earth shaking orgasm, just the feeling something was missing and a sore fanny for a couple of days. We muddled along, foreplay was always the same, I gave him a blow job, he tried to find my clitoris…the man needed a fucking map. Sex was nearly always missionary, I'd sneak on top whenever I could, but he'd always flip me over for a quick finish. Maybe we just became too familiar with each other but when he started to not take his socks off when we had a shag I knew it was time to move on. He wasn't that arsed to be honest, I think he'd started to prefer his games console to me anyway and if he could have stuck his knob in it I'm sure he would have dumped me before I dumped him. My relationship history since Hayden has been unremarkable, hence my decision to ditch the romance novels and dive head long, or should that be muff long, into Erotica.

I'm suppose you could say I'm reasonably pretty and my face is holding up well, which is surprising given my twenty a day smoking habit, absolute love of kebabs and a probable dependency on Prosecco. My tits aren't too bad, they measure in at a 36C and I'm pleased to say they are still nice and perky and probably a few years off resembling a Spaniel's ears. My legs are long and shapely and the cellulite on my arse can be hidden with a good, supportive pair of knickers. Thongs just aren't going to happen, sorry Erotica but negotiating with a piece of cheese wire up my arse does not do it for me whatsoever. I've been researching my subject well recently, and one of the first rules when embarking on an erotic adventure seems to be that one must have a shaven haven, a freshly mown lawn, a smooth muff…I think you get the picture. I need to think carefully about how I am going to achieve my erotica ready fanny as the expression 'bearded clam' doesn't describe the half of it!

I don't fancy having my fanny flaps waxed and shaving isn't really an option as I'm petrified I'll get a shaving rash. So the only option I've got is hair remover cream. A quick trip to the shops and it's mission accomplished; my lady garden is smothered in intimate hair remover cream. It looks like a Mr Whippy with sprinkles but definitely no chocolate flake. It's not the most attractive look in the world, I'm staggering around like a saddle sore old cowboy, but it's going to be worth it…I am Ann without an 'e' and without pubes, a bald fannied paragon of sexual liberation. That bird with the posh name in 50 shades of whatever is going to have nothing on me! Though I have to admit, the undercarriage was a bit of a nightmare and to be honest it does sting a bit. At least I don't have to wait too long and then I will be smooth, shiny and....ouch...I'm fucking burning now! Burning is not right surely? Jesus, my flaps are on fire. Give me a minute I need to jump in the shower and get this shit off.

I just spent four fucking hours in A&E. I washed the cream off and my minge was glowing red and burning like a bastard which was almost bearable until the swelling started. I could feel my lips starting to throb, they were pulsating like a rare steak. I didn't want to look down, but I knew I had to…fuck me I had testicles, just call me Johnny Big Bollocks because that is what I had. I quickly checked Dr Google and the best thing for swelling is elevation and an ice pack, so I spent the best part of half an hour with my minge in the air and a packet of frozen peas clamped between my thighs. Needless to say it had no effect at all and it became painfully clear that I was going to have to haul my now damp, swollen crotch to the hospital. Never before have I felt so humiliated, having to describe in intimate detail my problem to little Miss Smug Bitch at reception;

'So, you've come to A&E today because your vagina is swollen'...

…well it's my vulva actually but let's not split pubic hairs, or try and get them off with cunting hair remover cream. Sour face huffed and puffed and eventually booked me in, I spent what felt like an eternity pacing around…I couldn't sit down, my testicles wouldn't allow it and by this time a ball bra wouldn't have gone amiss. The Doctor I saw, who was absolutely gorgeous (the one time I didn't want to show an attractive man my fanny) and, when he wasn't stifling a laugh, couldn't have been more sympathetic. I'd had an allergic reaction and he'd prescribe me some anti-histamines which would bring the swelling down, my labia would return to their normal size and other than some skin sensitivity for a few days I would be fine but under no circumstances was I to use hair remover cream again as next time the reaction could be even worse. Though what could be worse than the whopping set of bollocks I'd grown I don't know. So that's that, I'm going to have to go au natural. Which is fine by me, I'd rather have a hairy beaver than an angry one.

A few hours later and my muff has more or less returned to normal and other than feeling slightly itchy seems to be perfectly fine. I've crossed shaven haven off my to do list and need to carry on with my preparation. As you may have already gathered, I've got a lot of work to do. I've noticed in most of the Erotica I've read that the words penis and vagina are rarely used, so I need to practise my sexual vocabulary, I need to learn how to talk dirty…I need to do my Erotica homework. I've had another flick through some of my books and there's no way I can call my vagina 'my sex' I know strictly speaking it is, but for fuck's sake…'my sex craves you', 'my sex needs your sex' it's all sounds a bit contrived if you ask me so I think I'll check out the Urban Dictionary.

I've just spent a good hour trawling through and my God what an education that was. Either I'm more wet behind the ears than I thought I was or some of the things I've just read are made up, check out 'Angry Pirate'…that's not for real, is it? I'm ready to try some of the new words and phrases I've learnt. I need to be all pouty lipped and doe eyed as I look in the mirror, moisten my lips and purr:

'I want to suck your length'

'Do you want to drink out of my cream bucket'

'My clit is hard and ready to be licked'

'My vagina is the most magical place in the world, come inside'

What the fuck was I thinking, I can't say this shit! Firstly the doe eyed, pouty lip thing makes me look like I'm pissed and secondly I can't do this without laughing. I'm much more comfortable with 'do you fancy a pint of Guinness and a quick shag'. I quickly give my head a wobble, comfortable is boring. I'm in this for the excitement and the clit tingling thrill (see I did learn something). Maybe I'll just opt for quiet and mysterious, let my body do the talking and my mouth do the sucking (I'm really starting to get this now). So that's the plan, my persona will be a sultry erotic goddess who doesn't say much, I'll be irresistible, a fabulous shag who doesn't want a conversation, no chat just sex.

The last part of my preparation is what on earth am I going to wear? If I'm going for the mysterious look does that mean I'm going to have to channel my inner sex goddess, or does it mean I go for a prim and proper, hair up, professional look? Maybe a combination of both, tight fitting dress, hair up and glasses, then I can do the whole taking my glasses off and flicking my hair down thing. The hair flicking thing however is a bit of an issue for me: my hair is naturally curly…really curly, at university my nickname was 'pube head' which probably tells you all you need to know, so I'm going to have to straighten it to within an inch of its life. From frump to fox…check me out. Today is going to be an exciting day. I'm just waiting for the postman to arrive, I've ordered some proper lingerie. I've gone for two sets initially, traditional black and racy red. Shit, should I have ordered a dildo? I forgot about a fucking dildo and candles, I forgot candles! What about a butt plug…what actually is a butt plug? I can't be erotic if I'm not dripping hot wax on him whilst pleasuring myself with a multi speed vibrating dildo…okay, so maybe not at the same time but you get my drift. Handcuffs! Shit, I'm not very good at this, he'll just have to tie me up with my big knickers.

The postman came, and I swear he had a knowing glint in his eye when he asked me to sign for my delivery or maybe he just read the label on the back of the parcel, cheeky bastard. It took me a while to build up the courage but here I am, standing in front of a full length mirror wearing a bright red, lacy push up bra, matching arse covering comfortable pants, a suspender belt and black stockings. I'm not sure. My tits are standing to attention and look like boiled eggs in a frilly egg cup, they are virtually dangling from my ear lobes and I swear you can see my minge stubble. So the new plan will be to go for subdued or even better, no lighting at all. I think it's all starting to look really erotic… bushy fanny, no filthy talking and everything done in the dark. The scene is set and I'm ready to get out there. No strings, erotic sex here I come. Well, not quite, I need to sign up to a dating site.

I take a selfie of myself looking as sultry as possible (not doe eyed or pouty, we know that doesn't work) I decide to show a little bit of cleavage and a little bit of leg, but not too much I want to leave my potential dates gagging to see more…I'm such a temptress. I've written and rewritten my profile about twenty times, it has to be just right and I think on my twenty first attempt I've finally done it:

'Flirty thirty two year old,

I work in marketing,

I like to get my head down in both the boardroom and the bedroom,

I'm looking for no strings attached fun,

Hobbies include reading, cooking and amateur dramatics.'

I know, you don't have to tell me, it's painfully shit. Hopefully they'll just look at my profile picture and to be honest at this point I don't care, I've submitted everything and I am now a fully paid up member of a dating site.

It takes a couple of hours for my phone to eventually ping with a notification that I have a message, I'm trembling with excitement as I open it…

'You've got nice tits'

Fuck me, 'You've got nice tits' is that it? I mean it's nice he thinks I've got nice tits, but I was expecting a little bit more. No, hang on he's sent a picture…it's a dick! He's sent me a picture of his dick, eww I don't think I've ever seen such a stumpy little penis, it's got a hugely bulbous bellend which looks like it's going to explode at any minute and hang on, it looks like it's winking at me…I'm never going to be able to unsee that! I quickly delete the message, when my phone pings again…It's another dick, not the same dick, this one is long, thin and veiny as fuck. Maybe I'm being too fussy, knobs aren't supposed to be attractive are they? My phone is quickly becoming a rogues gallery of ugly shlongs. I'm really starting to think maybe this wasn't a good idea, I know I said I wanted plenty of cock, but this wasn't exactly what I meant. Three cocks later and just as I am about to give up on the whole idea (maybe a pint of Guinness and a quick shag isn't too bad after all) I get a message from Daniel. I check out his profile and he actually looks quite fit, he's good looking, athletic and he didn't send me a dick pic....

What happens next?...buy the book to find out!

Go to Amazon and search Wax Whips and My Hairy Bits S J Carmine

And...while I still I have you here I'd like to recommend a book of short stories from my talented brother, Richard Hennerley, that are full of love, magic, triumph, tragedy and whimsy...the book is called 'Floating Away' and here's part of one of the tales from the book...

The Boy who was Strange and Different

<u>Part 1. Mother and Son.</u>

Once upon a time… many, many years ago in a world long since forgotten, there was a country called Anywhere. And in the land of Anywhere there was a fine and prosperous city called Anyplace and in this fine city lived a woman who had three children, two girls and a boy.

Unfortunately for the children The Woman was a person of inordinate selfishness, one of those people who feel that they world revolves around them and them alone, someone who was prepared to do anything to get what she wanted. To make things worse, the children had lost their father at an early age. The poor man had died of a broken heart for during the course of his marriage to The Woman he had come to realise that she had not married him for love but simply as a way of escaping from her own background (which had been rather Poor And Mean) and gaining Financial Security and Social Standing. For his own reasons, which to this day remain unfathomable, the husband had loved The Woman dearly and simply could not reconcile the love he felt for her with the total lack of love she had for him. So he succumbed to the Sadness Disease (which in your world you call cancer) but beat it to its fatal conclusion by drinking himself to death.

This left three children (another unfathomable that also remains unanswered to this day – exactly why did she have children?) to be raised by one very strange woman. The Woman only had two Real Loves and they were Social Standing and Gambling. She loved nothing more than praise and attention from friends, associates and The Neighbours and, in pursuit of such, would portray herself to those around her as a brave and valiant Single Mother who Devoted Her Life to raising and caring for her darling children, and such performance did indeed bring her much praise and her precious, desired Social Standing.

But The Woman's Truth as she presented it to the world was a Fiction. The Woman's children were left pretty much to bring up themselves, she was an Absent And Unconcerned parent for her love for herself and her needs was too great to spare any love for her children. She put food on the table and clothes on the children's backs but nothing else. And then not always, for almost every cent and penny that came into the household was spent on The Woman's other Great Love: gambling. Oh, how The Woman loved to gamble, for hours and days on end. She would gamble on horses, dogs, rabbits, flashing lights – anything that moved and presented a chance of a chance!

Growing up with this strange, self-obsessed woman was difficult for all three children but most particularly for The Boy. Girls are always cleverer about these things and The Boy's sisters had long since recognised The Mother for the Selfish And Uncaring creature she was and they had simply resolved to get on with life until such time as they were old enough to leave home and never come back. The Boy felt things more keenly for, like his father, he had, for yet another unfathomable reason to this day unexplained, a Deep And Abiding Love for his mother. And he desperately wanted her to return that love, to share a kind word, a warm embrace. Of course, The Woman never did any of these things but the more she showed The Boy that she had no love for him, the more he wanted her to love him and the harder he would try to be loved and he would say:

'Look at this, Mum',

'I love you, Mum',

'Look what we did at school today, Mum.'

'You look nice today, Mum.'

'I made this for you, Mum.'

And The Woman would grunt and turn her back on him and return to her gambling or telling stories to The Neighbours of her sacrifices for her children as a struggling Single Mother.

Truth be told, The Woman didn't just not love her son, she despised him. She saw him as a threat to her Social Standing for whilst The Boy had a pleasing and loving nature and was not unintelligent or untalented (indeed he had a beautiful singing voice) or unattractive, he was small for his fourteen years and had a certain gentle feyness about him – a degree of femininity that she disliked and distrusted. She was very concerned that the child might be a *falulah* (a 'falulah' is Anywhere slang that corresponds to words like 'queer' and 'faggot' in your world).

Now, this Tale is set in some years back in the history of Anywhere, before the brief Golden Age and social, cultural and economic blooming that occurred as a result of breaking the dead grip of The Greedy One Percent (sadly short-lived though that period was) and

Social Attitudes were, particularly on matters of difference and sexuality, still very retarded – being identified as a falulah was a matter of great Social Embarrassment and shame and it was widely considered that a person was better off dead than falulah. So- The Mother's suspicions that her son might be 'one of them' caused her considerable concern. Imagine the Social Shame of having a son who was inclined that way. What would the neighbours think? And the damage such shame would cause to her Social Standing! Unacceptable!

Then one day all The Woman's fears were confirmed for The Boy came back from school with a ripped shirt and a bloody lip and tears in his eyes. 'Mum,' he said, 'the other boys beat me and laughed at me and called me a falulah, why mum, why?'

And a spasm of pure terror and shame shot through The Woman. See, she had been right, the boy was a fulalah and now other people were beginning to notice! Oh, the shame, all those years of building up her Social Standing were going to be ruined by this horrible, useless falulah child.

'Well, I'm not surprised,' said the infuriated mother, 'I mean look at you, you're pathetic, you're so small, you're tiny compared to the other boys and you sound like a girl. Huh, they're right you are a falulah!' With these words she walked towards her child and The Boy, despite her harsh words, thought (or at least fervently hoped) that she was going to comfort him. Instead she stopped short of The Boy, raised a hand above her head and slammed it down with all her strength across his face, knocking him to the floor. 'Get upstairs to your room!' she screamed. And as the terrified child did just that, she screamed after him:

'Dwarf!'

'Midget!'

'Falulah!'

'Falulah!'

Calming herself, The Mother thought about what she should do. A falulah for a son, what a humiliation. She couldn't let this miserable child threaten her Social Standing – but short of murdering the child (which, to be quite frank, she would have done were it not for the fear of being caught) what could be done? And she thought. And she thought. And she thought. And she came up with a plan.

The next day, whilst The Boy was at school, she made her way to The Asylum For The Strange And The Different.

Part 2. The Asylum For The Strange And The Different.

To understand what happened next in this tale it is necessary to understand about The Asylum For The Strange And The Different and its position in Anywhere's society at this point in Anywhere's history. Fundamentally, it was a dumping ground – for The Strange and The Different – The Strange being those considered to be mad and The Different being those who didn't quite fit in with society because they perhaps had strange views and ideas, or whose politics were regarded as dangerous or who were, perhaps, falulahs.

Once an unfortunate individual was placed in The Asylum, that was it, They were gone. Lost. Invisible.

Never to be heard from again. No inmates of The Asylum ever left that grim place alive.

And The Asylum was truly dreadful, a black pit of madness and despair: those who worked there only worked there as a very last resort, out of desperation to earn some kind of living. Faeries would not fly within a two mile radius of it and Trolls would not even mention it in conversation (to do so was considered to bring the worst of luck): even Death was a reluctant to go there, though The Devil did think it rather a fun place to visit. Certainly nobody ever came to see anybody at The Asylum; after all it was where Strange or Difficult were dumped and why, having got rid of them, would one want to visit them?

Within the walls of The Asylum there was no concept of treatment or care for its reluctant inmates. The Different were there simply to keep their disturbing ideas and proclivities away from wider society – that was all, nothing to do but keep them locked away until they died. The Different – they were just mad and there was nothing to done about that: in the land of Anywhere at this time madness was considered not be an illness or dysfunction but an Altered State. The belief was that mad people were mad because they had, in some way, communed with The Devil. During the course of their congress with Satan, he had allowed them to open the pages of his Book Of The Dead. The Devil's Book Of The Dead is a kind of Satanic Stamp Album. An album of huge size and length in which The Devil, the Ultimate Connoisseur Of Suffering, records (for his delight and delectation) the saddest of deaths – those being to The Devil (and to your narrator) the premature deaths, be it by disease or violence, of The Young And The Innocent. And each death is recorded not in words, instead it is written in emotion, in the pain and sadness that was endured in the course of that death. As such, The Devil's Book Of Death contains a depth of pain so great, so deep, so profound that to open even one page for one second is enough to plunge any man or woman into madness, a madness that is pure and unchangeable – an Altered State. All that is to be done with a person who has peered into The Devil's Book Of Death is to assign them until death to The Asylum For The Strange And The Different.

So, there you have it, The Asylum For The Strange And The Different was no more or no less than a place where those considered mad, different, awkward or embarrassing were sent to die. Once in, there was no way out except death. To be an inmate in The Asylum was to 'live' in a state of non-existence.

Let's return now to my little tale. Having been informed of the nature and purpose of The Asylum For The Strange And The Different you've probably guessed the purpose of The Mother's visit there. That's right, she'd gone there to visit the Director of The Asylum to plead her case for having The Boy admitted (dumped and forgotten until death) there. All in all, things went well for her. The Director, a miserable bigot of a man who abhorred difference of any kind and particularly falulahs, had agreed with her. Her case was justified, keeping a falulah in the family home would indeed result in Unacceptable Embarrassment to her with a concomitant drop in her Social Status. However, just to oil the wheels, smooth the path and get The Boy admitted the next day might she consider a Small Token Of Her Appreciation, maybe just lie back and lift up her skirt, just twenty minutes of her time?

The Mother considered the Director's request to have sex with her and thought, why not if it's going to get the job done and get that horrible child out my life? The decision was made all the easier to make because on the way to The Asylum she had suddenly realised another 'plus' of getting rid of The Boy: one less mouth to feed would mean more money for one of the true loves of her life – gambling! Don't be shocked, I did tell you she was a truly awful woman…

The next day, The Boy was getting ready for school (The Boy and his sister's always got themselves ready for school, The Mother never being awake that early in the day due to having been up late gambling) when, much to his surprise his mother appeared, fully dressed, bright and smiling.

'Well hullo, my little man!' she said cheerily, 'and how are you today? My son, my beloved son, you've been having a difficult time so today there'll be no school – you're coming to the shops with me and we're going to buy you a treat and then we'll go for a lovely Sludge burger!'

And The Boy beamed from ear to ear, for this was Heaven to him, at last his mother was being nice to him, the only thing he really, really wanted in life was finally coming to pass!

The Boy and his mother jumped into a clarb (the Anywhere equivalent of a London black cab) and began their journey. The Mother explained to The Boy that before they went to the shops she just had to stop off somewhere and 'pick something up for a friend.' The Boy nodded and smiled and took hold of his mother's hand and squeezed it gently. This vaguely repulsed The Mother but she accepted it, even squeezed The Boy's hand gently back – keep the horrible little thing happy and quiet, she thought, I'll soon be rid of it, she thought.

By and by, the clarb came to, you've guessed it, The Asylum For The Strange And The Difficult, and the mother said 'come on, little man, come with me – this thing I have to collect is quite heavy so you can give me a hand!'

Willingly The Boy jumped out of the clarb with his mother, happy to help. Seeing the huge, grey, bleak, hulking building before him he felt a sense of doom and despair but comforted himself with the thought that he was with his mother, she'd make sure that everything was fine.

Into The Asylum went mother and soon. Down long, depressing corridors painted that sickly, pale shade of green beloved by bureaucracies in all worlds everywhere, until they came to a blank, anonymous looking door. 'Ah, yes,' said the mother, 'this is where we should be – be a dear and pop into this room will you and pick up the package there…' and she swung open that anonymous door. And The Boy, eager to please, entered the room and before he could register the fact that it contained no package, two burly Asylum employees threw a thick, heavy net over him and wrestled him to the ground, dragging him out of the room and down, down, down another long, depressing corridor and as he kicked and screamed and was hauled away to a state of non-existence oh, how the mother laughed and she shouted:

'Idiot!'

'Midget!'

'Girl!'

'Falulah!'

'Falulah!'

And The Boy cried:

'Mummy!'

'No, mummy, no!'

'Why, mummy?'

'Why?'

'Why....'

What happens next? Buy the book (available in Kindle and paperback formats) and find out!

Printed in Great Britain
by Amazon

84565528R00078